To my daughter, Aria,
may you always be happy, healthy, and
kind as you explore the universe.

No part of this book is to be duplicated or commercialized without explicit permission from the publisher.

Registered trademark & copyright © 2020 by GenBeam, LLC.
Book, cover and internal design by GenBeam, LLC.
Cover and internal illustrations © 2020 by GenBeam, LLC.
Published in the United States by GenBeam, LLC.
All rights reserved.

Visit us on the Web!
www.tinkertoddlers.com

Contact us!
tinkertoddlerbooks@gmail.com

Tinker Toddlers supports early STEM learning. STEM is an acronym for science, technology, engineering, and mathematics. We provide simple explanations about emerging STEM concepts to the littlest learners to help facilitate the absorption of complex details later in life.

Introducing STEM early has shown to improve aptitude in math, reading, writing and exploratory learning in a wide spectrum of topics.

Mars!
for Kids
Dr. Dhoot

Do you know what **planet** we live on?

It's a beautiful planet called Earth.

Mars is part of the solar system.
The solar system has 8 planets, including Earth.

Some planets are big, some are small,
some are rocky, and some are made of gas.

All 8 planets are different.

But Mars is most like Earth, even though it may not look like it.

Earth
7926 miles

Mars
4220 miles

Let's see how they are alike!

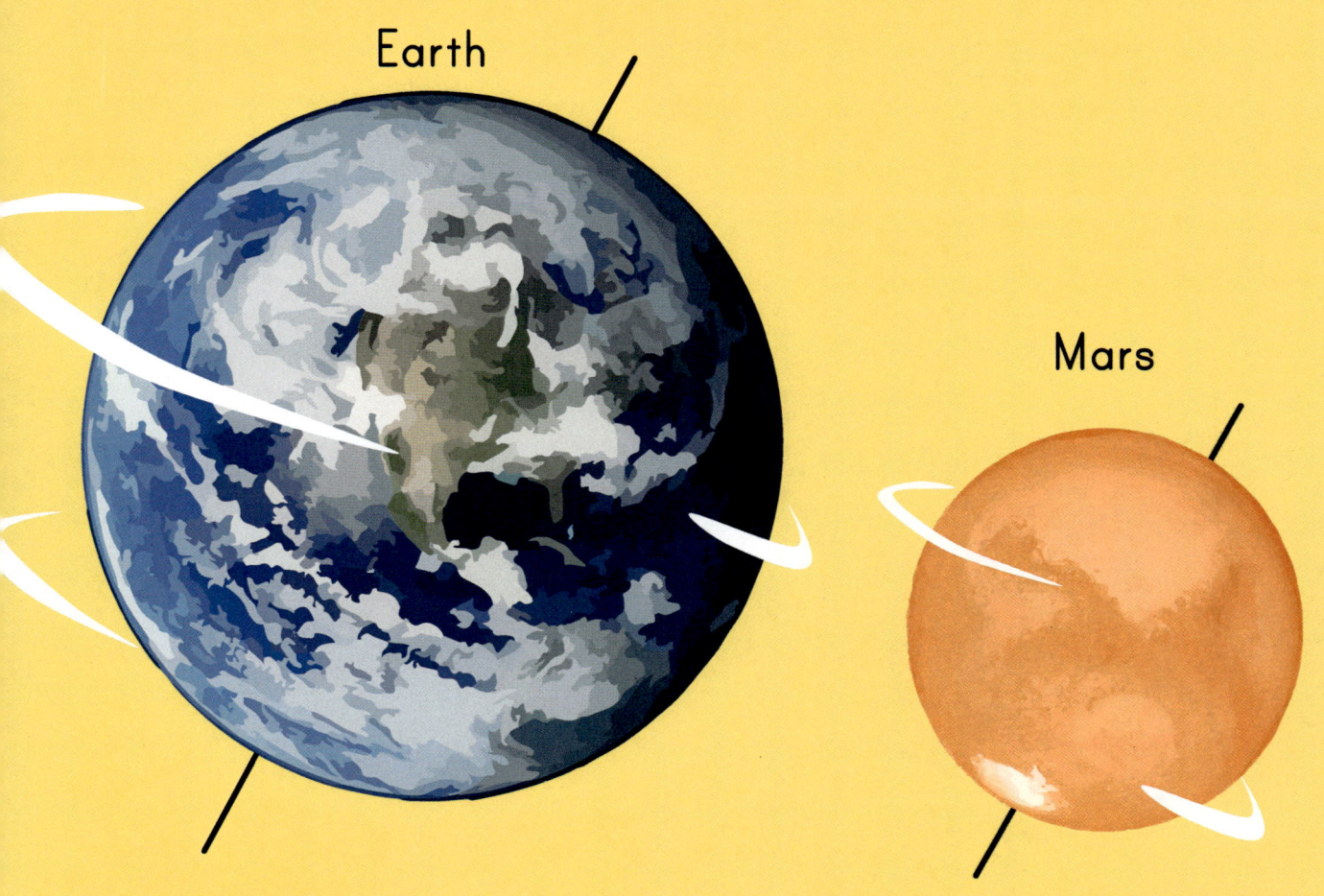

They also spend their
year the same way —

going around the Sun.

Although,
Mars takes a lot longer.

Days to go around the Sun:
Earth - averages 365 days
Mars - averages 687 days

Not all planets have **moons**.
But Earth and Mars do.

Moon

Mars has 2 moons.

Phobos

Deimos

...and Mars does too!

Mars has ice caps made of frozen water and frozen **carbon dioxide** at its north and south poles.

But it is frozen at the poles and underground.

Earth and Mars are also made of the same stuff on the inside.

Rock!

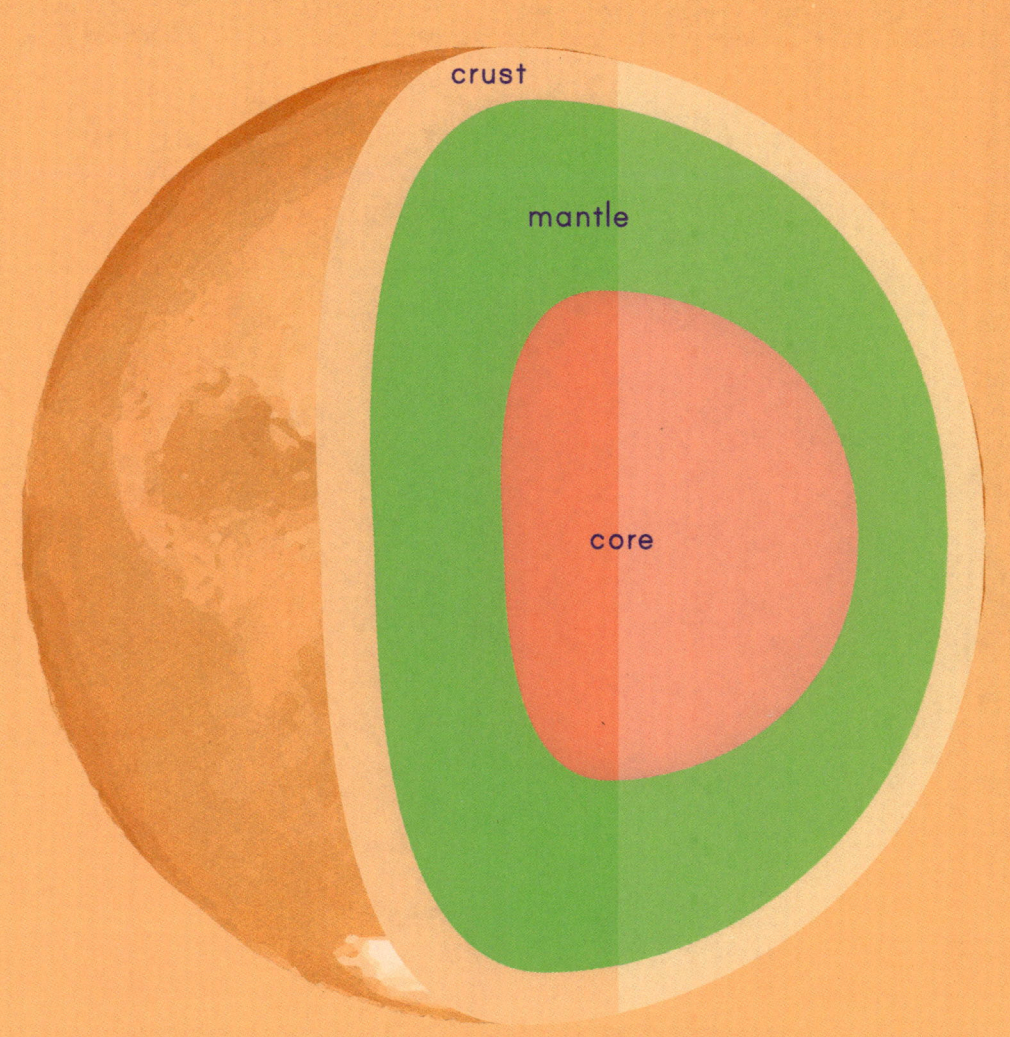

But, we can not live on Mars like we do on Earth. It is not **habitable.**

Viking Lander landed in 1976

Sojourner Rover landed in 1997

Spirit Rover landed in 2004

Mars Pathfinder landed in 1997

To learn more, we sent **robots**!

Phoenix landed in 2008

Curiosity Rover landed in 2012

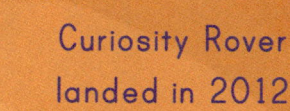

Opportunity Rover landed in 2004

Insight landed in 2018

But to learn even more,
we need to go to Mars ourselves.

The trip can take a while, as long as 8 months.

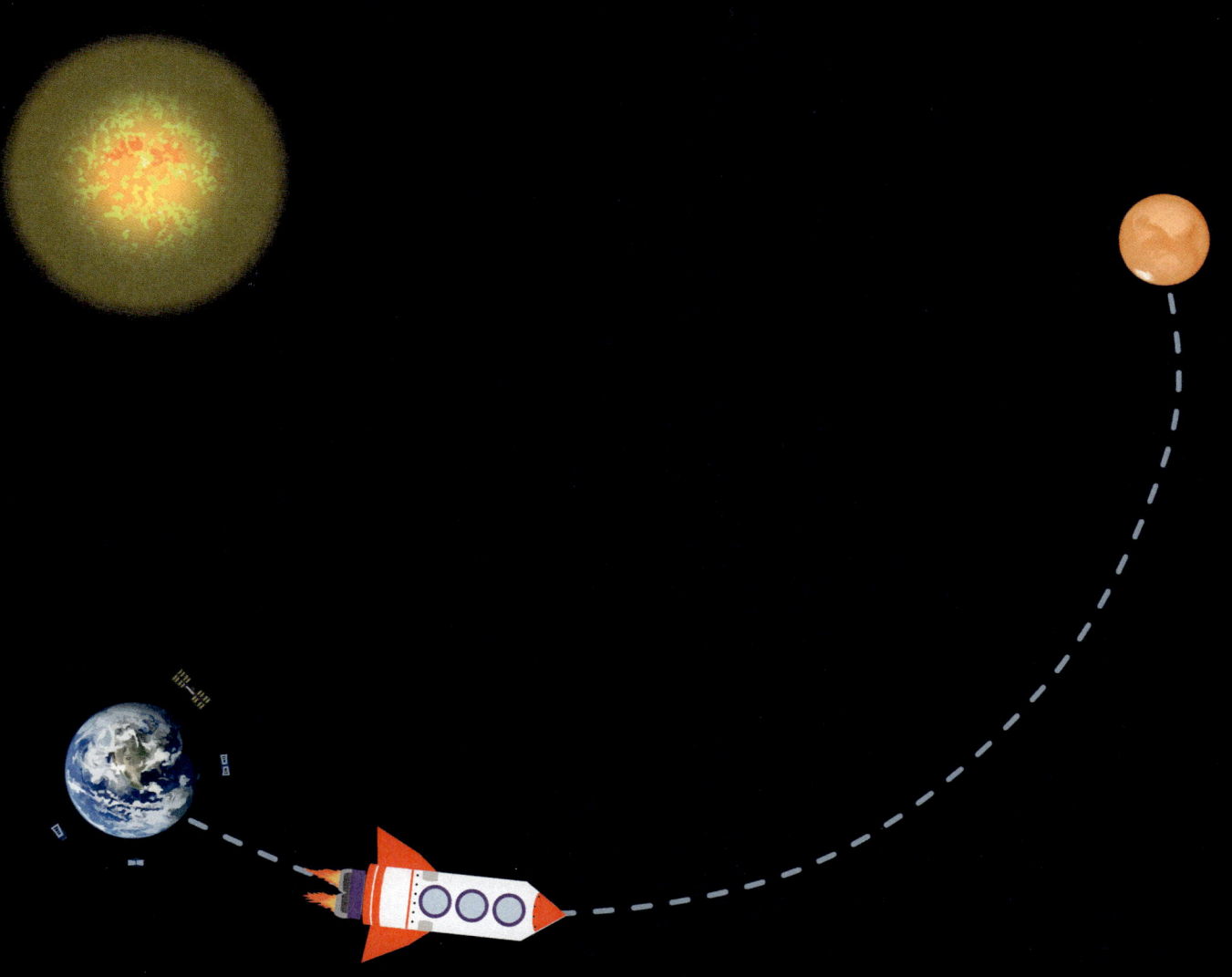

We will go to Mars in **rockets**!

These are **spaceships**!

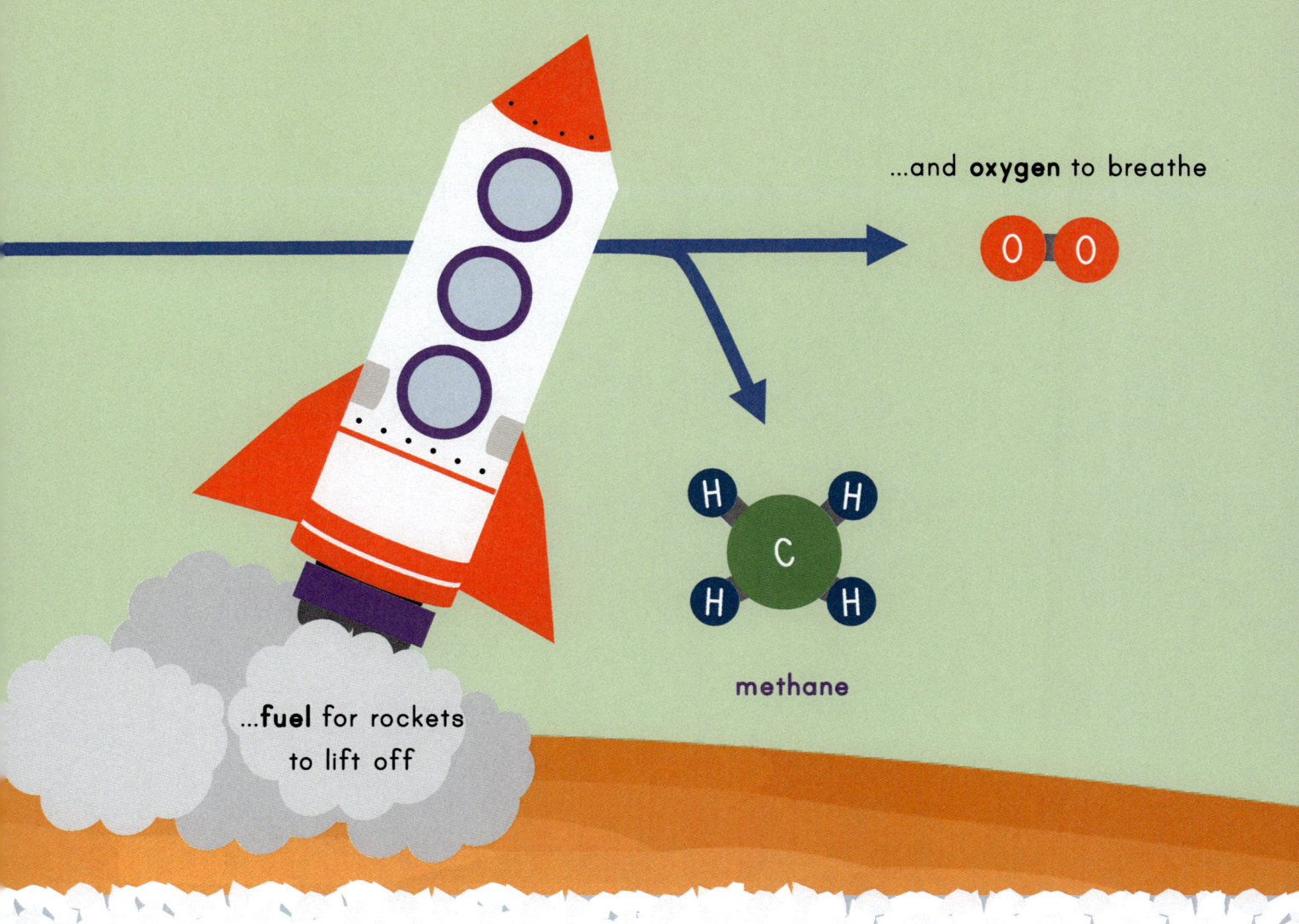

A **spacesuit** will keep us safe while we learn.

It will protect us.

A spacesuit provides oxygen,

controls temperature,

and protects you from **radiation**.

We'll have to bring our own food.

It will take time for plants to grow.

Glossary

Carbon Dioxide: Mars has a lot of this gas. It has no color or smell. Earth's air has about 0.04% carbon dioxide. Mars has 95% carbon dioxide. It can be converted to oxygen and fuel.

Earth: The planet on which we live. It is the third planet from the Sun.

Fuel: A material that is burned to produce heat power or thrust. We need fuel to make rockets go. **Methane**, CH_4, is the fuel that can be made from carbon dioxide and water.

Habitable: Suitable or fit to live in.

Interplanetary: To travel between planets.

Mars: The fourth planet from the Sun. Also known as 'rusty' or the 'Martian' planet.

Moon: A large round object that circles around something other than a star. Earth has one moon.

Oxygen: A gas we need to live. It has no color or smell. Earth's air has about 20% oxygen. Mars has 0.14% oxygen.

Planet: A large body in outer space that circles around a sun. We have 8 planets in our solar system.

Radiation: A form of energy used in x-rays at the doctor's office. This energy can also harm you. The energy is radiated in the form of rays, waves, or particles.

Robot: A machine that can perform some of the same tasks as a human being.

Rocket: A flying device that is shaped like a tube. It is driven by hot gases released from engines in its bottom.

Solar System: Our Sun, its 8 planets, their moons, and all the bodies that travel around the Sun.

Spaceship: A vehicle that carries people or cargo in outer space. A spaceship takes us to the moon or other planets.

Spacesuit: A suit worn by astronauts that lets them breathe in outer space.

Water: A clear liquid with no taste or odor. Most life needs water to survive. Rain comes from rain, rivers, oceans, and lakes.

Questions for your little traveler

We live in the Milky Way Galaxy.
Look up at the night sky. How many stars can you see? Can you see our galaxy?

We are gearing up to go to Mars.
Why do you think we should go there?

We will journey to Mars using rockets!
If you had a rocket, what would it look like?

Draw it out on the next page and share it by posting a review!

My Rocket

To share, go to order history at place of purchase, locate product, and click on "write a product review"!

Dear Reader,

I hope that you enjoyed learning about Mars! I am excited to become an interplanetary species, and hope you are too!

Science and technology are evolving rapidly and it can be hard to keep up. I hope you and your little learner(s) enjoy learning the very basics and continue to build on them.

If you liked this story and want to read more like it, there is a whole series of Tinker Toddlers books on Amazon, just waiting for you.

Best,

Dr. Daoot

www.TinkerToddlers.com
tinkertoddlerbooks@gmail.com

Tinker Toddlers' Growing Library

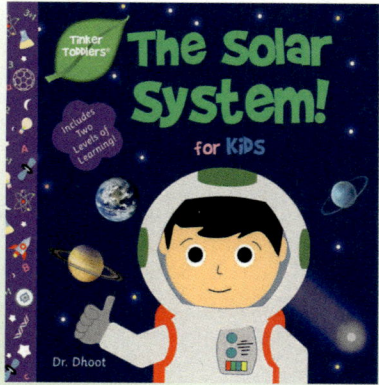
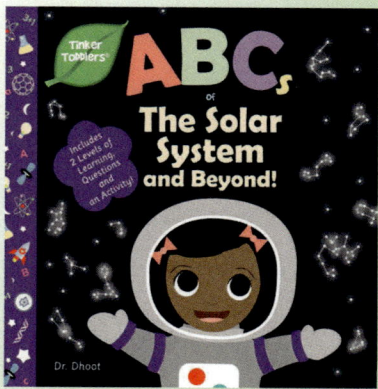

amazon.com/author/drdhoot

tinkertoddlerbooks@gmail.com

Industry experts, scientists, engineers,
parents, and kids contribute much of their time to ensure
Tinker Toddlers is successful at supporting early STEM learning.

To support our efforts, please:

1) go to order history at place of purchase
2) locate product
3) click on "write a product review"
4) tell us what your favorite part was

Made in the USA
Monee, IL
08 June 2021